ME, TOMA AND THE CONCRETE GARDEN

Andrew Larsen

Anne Villeneuve

Kids Can Press

There's a box of dirt balls on my aunt Mimi's balcony, which is kind of weird if you ask me.

"Why do you have dirt balls out here?" I ask her.

"They were a present from a secret admirer," she says, with a twinkle in her eye. "I was hoping they'd be chocolates. I still don't know what to do with them."

"Are you sure this secret person even likes you?" I say. "They gave you a box of dirt!"

We both burst out laughing at the thought of it.

I'm staying with Mimi for most of the summer. My mom had an operation. It's nothing serious, but she has to take it easy for a while.

When I arrived at Mimi's, she said we could paint the guest room. I got to choose the color. But I couldn't decide, so she let me choose two. We painted stripes!

Most everything else is pretty gray around here, though, and it
doesn't look like it will be much of a summer. I already miss home.

One day I notice a kid throwing a ball against the tall brick wall by the empty lot. He looks up and waves.

"Why don't you wave back?" Mimi asks.

"I don't even know him," I tell her.

"Not yet ..." she says.

When I see the kid out there again the next day, I grab as many dirt balls as I can hold and run downstairs.

"Do you want to throw some dirt balls with me?" I ask him when I get to the tall brick wall.

"Dirt balls?" he asks back.

"My aunt said she'd pay us to get rid of these," I explain. "We can throw them into the empty lot. Then we can get some ice cream. Want to?"

"I guess," says the boy, a little unsure. "You live around here?"

"I'm staying with my aunt," I say, pointing to Mimi's balcony. "I'm Vincent."

"I live over there," he says, pointing to a balcony a few floors above Mimi's. "I'm Toma."

The dirt balls sail over the tall brick wall and land in the empty lot.

When we've pitched the last of them, we throw Toma's ball against the wall and try to catch it as it bounces back. We get up to forty-two catches without dropping it.

"Do you want some ice cream?" I ask.

"Sounds good," he says. "It's hot out here."

We head over to the ice cream truck parked in front of the
building.

Toma gets chocolate. I get strawberry.

Toma tells me about some of the other kids from his
neighborhood.

I tell him about some of the kids from mine.

We make a plan to meet up again to throw more dirt balls.

"Hey!" shouts a grumpy-looking man, watering the plants on his balcony the next day. "What are you kids throwing into that lot?"

"Dirt balls," I answer.

The man looks surprised.

"What's with Mr. Grumpypants?" Toma says to me as he throws the last of the dirt balls.

"Maybe he thinks we're littering," I suggest.

"But we're actually recycling," Toma says with a grin. "We're putting the dirt back where it belongs. He should be happy."

Toma and I meet by the tall brick wall almost every morning. Our new record for throwing the ball against the wall and catching it without dropping it is ninety-five. It won't be long before we crack one hundred.

And we read lots of comics. Toma has a huge collection.

We often see Mr. Grumpypants on his balcony, watering his plants.
Sometimes Mimi gives us money for ice cream. Toma always gets
chocolate. I always get strawberry.
The days fly by.

On rainy days like today, Toma and I usually hang out at Mimi's.
And as usual, there's Mr. Grumpypants on his balcony. But
today for some reason, he's waving at us and pointing to the
empty lot below.

We look down.

It's green!

"So there was something special about those dirt balls after all!"
Mimi says with a laugh.

"They must have had seeds in them!" I say.

"What kind of seeds?" asks Toma.
"I guess we'll know soon enough," says Mimi.
Across the way, Mr. Grumpypants is giving us a big thumbs-up.
We give him three thumbs-up back.

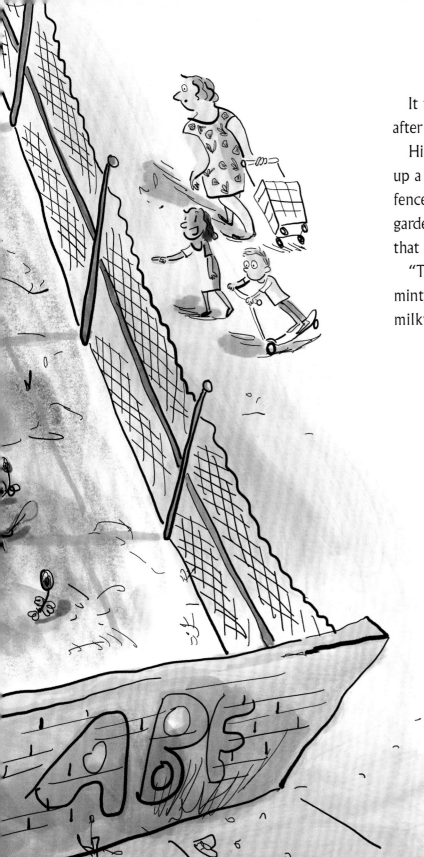

It turns out that Mr. Grumpypants isn't so grumpy after all.

His name is Marco. He helps Toma and me hook up a hose so we can water the garden through the fence every morning. And he knows a lot about gardening. He teaches us the names of the flowers that are starting to grow.

"There's crimson clover, snapdragon, poppy, lemon mint, black-eyed Susan," he says. "There's even some milkweed. Butterflies are going to love it here!"

Marco is right.

Butterflies flock to our garden.

"I have some good news, Vincent," says Mimi one afternoon, putting her arms around me. "I was just talking with your mom. She's feeling much better. She's coming to bring you home this weekend."

"But who'll take care of the garden?" I say.

"We all will," says Mimi, with a squeeze. "I promise. And you can come back to visit next summer."

I'm really happy my mom is better, but there's a little part of me that's sad.

I'll miss Mimi and Toma.

I'll probably even miss Marco.

A year feels like a long time …

But finally it's summer again. My mom and I are staying with
Mimi for a little vacation. We're calling her place Camp Mimi.
   I brought Mimi a box of chocolates.
   And I brought some seeds. Toma and I are going to make
our own dirt balls.

We're going to see what else we can grow.

This book is dedicated to the students and teachers of Moraine Hills Public School in Richmond Hill, Ontario, with special thanks to Lori Drawetz — A.L.

To Jasmine. For all those blissful moments we spent wandering in the city. — A.V.

Text © 2019 Andrew Larsen
Illustrations © 2019 Anne Villeneuve

All rights reserved. No part of this publication may be reproduced, stored in a retrieval system or transmitted, in any form or by any means, without the prior written permission of Kids Can Press Ltd. or, in case of photocopying or other reprographic copying, a license from The Canadian Copyright Licensing Agency (Access Copyright). For an Access Copyright license, visit www.accesscopyright.ca or call toll free to 1-800-893-5777.

Kids Can Press gratefully acknowledges the financial support of the Government of Ontario, through the Ontario Media Development Corporation; the Ontario Arts Council; the Canada Council for the Arts; and the Government of Canada for our publishing activity.

Published in Canada and the U.S. by Kids Can Press Ltd.
25 Dockside Drive, Toronto, ON M5A 0B5

Kids Can Press is a Corus Entertainment Inc. company

www.kidscanpress.com

The artwork in this book was rendered in ink and watercolor.
The text is set in Albertus.

Edited by Yvette Ghione
Designed by Marie Bartholomew

Printed and bound in Shenzhen, China, in 10/2018 by C & C Offset

CM 19 0 9 8 7 6 5 4 3 2 1

Library and Archives Canada Cataloguing in Publication

Larsen, Andrew, 1960–, author
        Me, Toma and the concrete garden / written by Andrew Larsen ; illustrated by Anne Villeneuve.

ISBN 978-1-77138-917-4 (hardcover)

I. Villeneuve, Anne, illustrator II. Title.

PS8623.A77M4 2019   jC813'.6   C2018-904154-4